HAPPY WINTER

HAPPY WINTER

Karen Gundersheimer

A Harper Trophy Book

Harper & Row, Publishers

Love to Werner

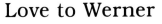

Happy Winter

Copyright © 1982 by Karen Gundersheimer

All rights reserved.

Printed in the United States of America.

Library of Congress Cataloging in Publication Data
Gundersheimer, Karen.
  Happy winter.

  Summary: Two sisters find very familiar activities
are transformed by the wonder of snowy days.

  [1. Stories in rhyme.   2. Winter—Fiction]   I. Title.
PZ8.3.G955Hap   1982   [E]   81-48650
ISBN 0-06-022172-0   AACR2
ISBN 0-06-022173-9 (lib. bdg.)

  (A Harper Trophy book)
ISBN 0-06-443151-7

First Harper Trophy edition, 1987.

CONTENTS

Happy Winter, rise and shine!

I love the early morning time.

My sister snuggles close to me —

Two bugs in a rug, we laugh and see

How frosty patterns look like lace —

Each window has its special face.

We rub the glass — Hey, look out there!

Surprise! Surprise! Snow's everywhere!

And everything's so twinkly bright —

Hooray for snow that fell last night!

Happy Winter, time to guess —

Eggs or muffins? Pancakes? — Yes!

We hurry out and take a seat,

The tea is hot, the juice is sweet,

Then drizzle syrup, start to eat

The best of any breakfast treat.

Happy Winter, get-dressed song —

I wish it didn't take so long

To wriggle into old snowsuits,

To lace and hook the rubber boots,

To zip and snap to keep things on

Or find a glove when mitten's gone.

Just tie the scarf around once more,

Then turn the knob, unlatch the door

And waddle, fat, in bulky clothes

Outside — It's cold! Wind stings my nose!

Happy Winter, shout and laugh!

I'll be the first to stomp a path

So follow me — my boots make tracks

That wind about and double back

To one smooth place of sparkly snow

13

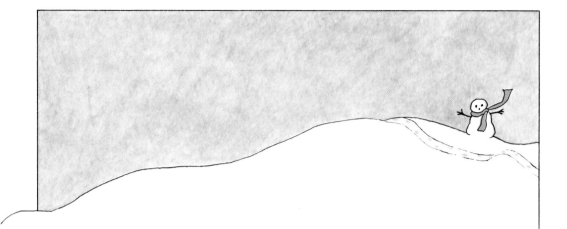

Then plop! Spread arms and legs like so

To make an angel shape — Come see!

My angel's just the size of me!

Now look at this — I'm going to take

A little twig and try to make

Each letter of my name in snow

So anyone who comes will know

I made that angel, boot marks, too,

And went back home when I was through.

Happy Winter, time to stay

Indoors on sleety, ice-cold days.

It's always fun when there's a friend

To hide-and-seek with, make pretend.

My quilt can be our tumbling mat.

We're famous circus acrobats

Who cartwheel in the center ring,

Who somersault and even sing.

We clap and bow, then run to bring

The box with all the dress-up things.

We try high heels and swishy skirts,

The wig, moustache and cowboy shirt.

And giggle, wiggle — wear the sheet —

This monster-ghost has six bare feet!

21

Happy Winter, time to bake

Some really yummy kind of cake.

So Mama flips through recipes

Just like she does for company

And reads them all — her favorite ones

Are Sunshine, Marble, Angel, Crumb.

But we pick Fudge, and no nuts, please —

Now tie on aprons, roll up sleeves.

23

The butter,  sugar, eggs go in

A mixing bowl, then beaters spin

To stir up yogurt, thick and sour,

With baking chocolate, salt and flour.

The batter's made, the oven's set,

The cake's popped in, and then we get

To scrape the bowl and beaters, too —

Last licks for me and slurps for you.

The timer pings! The cake is done —

Let's slice it up and all have some.

HAPPY WINTER FUDGE CAKE

Please ask a grown-up to help you make this yummy cake.

1. Preheat oven to 350° F.
2. Grease tube pan (9½″ x 3″).
3. Cut up 3 squares semisweet baking chocolate. Melt over very low heat or in double boiler. DO NOT BURN. Set aside to cool.
4. Get a medium-size bowl and mix dry ingredients (with wooden spoon):

   > 2 cups all-purpose flour
   > 1 cup sugar
   > 1 teaspoon baking soda
   > 1 teaspoon baking powder
   > Pinch of salt

5. Get a big bowl and mix wet ingredients (with electric mixer):

   > 2 eggs
   > ¼ cup soft butter or margarine, cut into small bits
   > 1 teaspoon vanilla
   > 1½ cups plain yogurt
   > Cooled melted chocolate (from 3 above)

6. Slowly add dry ingredients to wet ingredients, stirring with spoon to blend.
7. Add 1 cup chocolate chips. Stir them all in.
8. Pour batter into greased pan and place in preheated oven (350° F.)
9. Bake for 45 minutes or until cake tester or toothpick comes out clean. Cake may need another 5 minutes.
10. Let cool 30 minutes before turning out onto plate.
11. Slice it up and enjoy!

Happy Winter, let it snow!

It's almost Mama's birthday so

We're making presents. Shut the door!

Spread lots of paper on the floor.

Our hands get messy, wet and gray

From scrunching lumps of gucky clay,

Except we really try today

To make real things, so let's not play.

Aha! A bird!  You do the nest.

A homemade present's always best.

Quick, find a ribbon, wrap the box,

Then shove it underneath the socks —

But never tell, so no one knows

What secret hiding place we chose.

Happy Winter, time to read —

A pile of books is all I need.

My cat curls up to stay with me

And settles down to sleep or see

The pictures with the fairy tales —

Where Hansel leaves his breadcrumb trail,

Then magic spells make carpets sail

Or broomsticks carry water pails.

Some spooky stories give me shivers —

Witches haunt the hills and rivers!

Shipwrecks  smash on jungle coasts —

To read while munching buttered toast.

I like to try new books sometimes

But always love the nonsense rhymes

And tell my cat one *I* made up,

While sipping cocoa from a cup.

Happy Winter, steamy tub

To soak and splash in, wash and rub.

Big blobs of bubbles pile on me

The way the snow sits on a tree.

I rinse the soap off, scrub some more,

Drip puddles on the bathroom floor—

Then gurgling bubbles drain away,

A wet and merry end of day.

Happy Winter, evening time —

I like how little star-specks shine

Or blink and sparkle cheerfully —

They almost seem to wink at me.

And now switch on the bedside light
To shoo away the dark of night.

We read until we yawn, and then

With one last flick it's dark again.

The big black night is soft and spread

Just like the quilt upon my bed.

I'm warm and toasty, very snug,

Then Mama comes for one last hug

And sings a winter lullaby,

"Hush and quiet, close your eyes,

The moon's a night-light for the sky,

Where sprinkled stars are twinkling high

And far below, the deep drifts lie

'Til Northwind spins and flurries fly.

A snowy blanket's tucked in tight

And so are you, and now good night.

A happy winter day is done,

Now close your eyes and dreams will come."